THE MANHATTAN
MENACE

By W. A. Sorrells

Illustrations by
Tom Bancroft and Rob Corley

Published by KidsGive, LLC
5757 W. Century Blvd., Suite 800, Box 8
Los Angeles, California 90045

Karito Kids™ and KidsGive™ are trademarks of KidsGive, LLC.

Cover art by Funny Pages Productions, LLC (Tom Bancroft,
Rob Corley, and Jon Conkling)
Interior illustrations by Funny Pages Productions, LLC
(Tom Bancroft and Rob Corley)
Journal created by Wendy Tigerman
Interior design by Andrea Reider, Reider Publishing Services
Manuscript consulting by Shoreline Publishing Group LLC

ISBN-13: 978-0-9792912-3-4

Printed in China. First printing, 2007.

Visit Karito Kids at karitokids.com.

The first books in the series of Karito Kids™ Adventures are dedicated to Steve and Jeff for their constant support and belief in KidsGive; Hannah and Will for their enthusiasm for KidsGive's goal of helping children around the world; Dave for his commitment and friendship; Andrea for her awesome work and dedication; Janet for her humor and belief in us; and last, but most certainly not least, Julie for her spirit and chutzpah. We couldn't have done it without you. Thank you for helping us imagine, create, and become.

—Love, Laura and Lisa

Your Code Number is 895572001087.

MORE THAN JUST A BOOK
Find Out All The Ways To Enjoy This Mystery Adventure

Each Karito Kids™ Adventure is much more than simply a book. By reading this book and visiting karitokids.com, you can explore countries, solve mysteries, and best of all help kids in need in other parts of the world. Get to know all the Karito Kids and become a part of an exciting new community of kids who care!

1. **Activate Your Charitable Donation.** If you purchased this book with a Karito Kids Doll, you may have already activated your donation. If you purchased this book by itself, go to karitokids.com and follow the online instructions to activate your donation. Three percent of the price of this book will be donated by KidsGive on your behalf to the children's charity Plan. The best part is that you will get to choose the cause to which you want your donation to go. You decide how you want to make a difference!

2. **Go to karitokids.com.** Check out our Karito Kids Book Blog where you can learn more about your favorite characters, where they live, and other fun stuff. You can even share what you think about each adventure, the actions they took, and the choices they made. You can find out what other kids think, too!

3. **Look For Culture Crossings.** While you're reading this story, keep your eyes open for places in the book where another country or culture is mentioned. Located within the story, illustrations, or journal, these places are called "Culture Crossings." When you locate a place in the book where another country (other than the country the story is about) is mentioned, go to karitokids. com and visit the "Culture Crossings" area and follow the online instructions. As with all Karito Kids games, you will also earn virtual *World Change* that can be accumulated and then donated by KidsGive on your behalf (as real money) to Plan. You might also find a few surprises!

4. **Solve Hidden Quests.** Each Karito Kid has so many adventures to share. Log onto karitokids.com and visit the "Hidden Quest" area to join her on additional quests. Just as with "Culture Crossings," you can earn virtual *World Change* that can be accumulated and donated by KidsGive on your behalf (as real money) to Plan.

Join up with other kids who are *Playing for World Change!*~sm~

WHAT IS KARITO KIDS™ ALL ABOUT?

We launched Karito Kids™ to help connect children around the world in a number of ways.

◎ The word "Karito" means charity and love of one's neighbor in the constructed language Esperanto. We hope that children around the world strengthen their connection with each other, creating a global village of peace and understanding.

◎ Each Karito Kids Doll helps children recognize and appreciate the beauty of the world's many different ethnicities.

◎ The book that accompanies each Karito Kid tells a fun story involving that girl. It brings to life another country and its culture and connects readers to the notion that children from across the world have many fundamental similarities.

◎ The unique online activation process will allow children to directly participate in giving. They can determine the cause to which they wish to direct a percentage of the purchase price of the product. They can receive updates on the project they choose and find out how they helped children somewhere else in the world.

◎ Combining traditional play with innovative interactive games provides your child a play date with kids all over the world. They will have the opportunity to write to children sponsored by KidsGive and learn how children live in other parts of the world.

◎ Our selected charity, Plan, is a non-profit organization that is bringing hope and help to more than 10 million children and their families in poor communities worldwide. KidsGive contributes 3% of the retail price to one charity to maximize the impact of change.

even days," my mom said wearily, throwing her handbag onto the table of our tiny living room.

Honestly? I wasn't really paying attention. I was writing a song. "What rhymes with goofy?" I asked, strumming a chord on my guitar.

"Zoe Linden, did you hear me?" Mom said, sinking onto the couch. "It's all over in seven days."

I had no idea what she was talking about. "Some people say that I am goofy," I sang loudly, pounding out the chords on my guitar, "But at least I don't wear sleeves that are poofy." I frowned. Hmm. That wasn't so good.

"We're going to have to move out!" Mom said.

I looked up from my guitar, "Out of what?"

"Our house."

I stared. "Huh?"

"There's a lot I haven't told you," Mom said, her voice softening.

I put down my guitar. Mom had been acting

kind of weird lately. But now I was getting worried.

"Well, you know that before your father died," Mom said, "we bought that brownstone across the street. We wanted to fix it up and sell it. But things haven't worked out."

"Why not?"

"It's complicated." She sighed loudly. "The fact is, I've had to spend a lot of money. Designs, permits, lawyers. It's hard to explain. The bottom line is, I thought I was going to be able to do it. But I just totally ran out of money."

"Well, can't you get some more?"

Mom looked up at the ceiling. "I never told you what was going on because I didn't want you worrying. But the fact is, I'm broke. That famous real estate developer, Barrington Smith, wants our brownstone so that he can flatten that whole block and put up an apartment building. And we're going to lose this place, too, because the rents will be raised sky-high at the same time."

"What are we going to do?" Suddenly I had visions of me and Mom living in a cardboard box on some heating vent over on Broadway.

Mom sighed. "I guess we'll move back to my parents' house for a while."

Wait a minute! I was thinking. *Granny and*

Papa Jim live in Utica. That's about 250 miles north of here! Was she suggesting we were about to leave New York City? That was totally not possible! I'd lived in Greenwich Village, right here in the heart of downtown New York, for forever. This was my home! "But . . . can't you do something?"

"Honey, I need a hundred thousand dollars to finish paying off the loan on that house by tomorrow at five o'clock. I thought I was going to be able to borrow it from somebody. But that fell through today. It's just not going to happen."

My mother usually looked so beautiful and put together. But now she just looked tired and worn out.

"What if I made you a one-eyed egg sandwich?" I asked. "That'll make you feel better!" One-eyed egg sandwiches were the only thing I knew how to cook. But they always seemed to make Mom happy.

Only this time, Mom just sat there staring at the wall. "We're leaving the Village next week, Zoe," she said finally. "You might as well start packing your things."

Next week. It wasn't possible!

CHAPTER TWO

After my conversation with Mom, I ran up the stairs and pounded on Hana's door. My upstairs neighbor, Hana Kenyatta, is the same age as me, eleven. She's also my best friend. The Kenyattas rent the upstairs of the house. Hana's mother died when the World Trade Center was attacked on September 11, 2001. They're from Kenya, and her mom was working for an international law firm in one of the towers. So, like me, she has only one parent who's still alive.

Mr. Kenyatta answered the door holding a bunch of little paint brushes in his hand. He's an artist who paints pictures for kids' books. "Hi, Zoe," he said in his deep voice. Hana's father is a tall man with dark skin and a permanent smile on his face. "Hana!" he called over his shoulder. "Sunshine's here!" That's his nickname for me.

Hana came to the door. She's a short, serious-looking girl with very black skin and hair that she always pulls back in a ponytail. As usual, she had her skateboard in her hand. She never goes anywhere without her skateboard. "Let's go!" Hana said. She thundered down the stairs before I had a chance to say anything.

"Bye, Mr. Kenyatta!" I said, then I ran down the stairs, following Hana out to the street.

"Where should we go?" Hana asked.

"Hold on, hold on," I said, grabbing her arm. "I have totally the most crapalacious news in the history of the world."

Hana stopped and looked at me curiously. "Crapalacious? I believe that's another Zoism."

I tend to make up words. Hana calls them Zoisms. "It means totally, totally, totally horrible and bad and miserable," I said.

"I figured," Hana said. "So what's the crapalacious news?"

"We're going to have to move."

"Who is?"

"All of us." I explained what Mom had told me about having to sell the house and move.

"Barrington Smith is building apartments? Right over there?" Hana pointed at the brick house Mom owned. "*The* Barrington Smith?"

I nodded. Barrington Smith was pretty famous.

Hana scratched her head. "No," she said. "That's not gonna work. You just can't leave."

"But Mom says —"

"I'm going to have to put my genius brain to work on this," Hana said.

"Unless you have a hundred thousand dollars, that is," I said.

Hana looked at the brick house across the street. There was a tree sticking out of the top that must have been growing in the backyard. It was kind of unusual, because hardly anybody has a backyard in this part of New York City.

"We need more data," Hana said. Hana wants to be a scientist when she grows up, so she's always saying stuff like that. "I think we need to make an empirical study of the evidence."

"Huh?" I asked. "What's that mean?"

Hana lowered her voice and grinned at me. "We need to sneak into that old brownstone."

"Oh!" I said. "Why didn't you say so? I'm sure Mom has the key."

"No Entry!" the sign said. "By Order of the Fire Marshal."

I took out the grimy brass key I'd taken from Mom's key ring, inserted it into the lock and twisted. The way the paper sign was attached to the building, I had to tear it to open the door.

"Oops!" I said, giggling as the sign made this giant *RRRRRRRRRRrippp!* sound.

Hana followed me into the building. I slammed the door shut and looked around. "Wow!" I said. I knew Mom and Dad had bought this building two or three years ago, right before Dad got really sick with cancer. But I'd never been inside. Dad said I couldn't go inside because it was "structurally unsound." Which, I think, meant it was dangerous.

I was surprised to see the house was still full of furniture. Dust and cobwebs covered everything. It was real dark, too. Hana flicked the light switch on the wall, but it didn't do anything.

I switched on the flashlight I'd brought and shined it around the dark room.

There were still pictures hanging on the walls—ancient black-and-white photographs of men in high-collared shirts and women with impossibly tiny waists and feathered hats. Usually in old pictures people looked stiff and forbidding. But these people were all smiling, their eyes crinkled like they had been photographed in the middle of telling a joke. They looked like fun

people. One of the pictures showed a family of three — a woman with a huge pile of dark hair held in place by a sparkling tiara, a man wearing a top hat with a large mustache and a gold-headed cane, and a girl who looked so much like me she could have been me. It was so weird!

Just like me, she had long, curly, blonde hair. Just like me, she was smiling. And she had to have been about my age, too. Only she was wearing an old-fashioned white lace dress and white stockings and black patent-leather shoes. Everyone in the family was holding their arms out like, *Ta-daaaaa!*

Hana stood next to me and looked at the picture, too. "Whoa! Look at the crown that lady's wearing. You think she was a queen or something?"

"Tiara," I said. "It's a *tiara*." I know this partly because I know everything about stuff you put on your head. You see, I love hats of all kinds. I get them all over — flea markets, second-hand stores . . . .

"Oh, yeah, I guess you're right." Hana squinted at the picture. "Still, look at all those diamonds! I bet that would be worth a trillion bucks."

I looked closer at the woman. It really was a beautiful piece of jewelry, sparkling with dozens of diamonds.

Hana quickly lost interest in the tiara. "This is *so* cool!" she said. She dropped her skateboard on the floor and skated across the living room. The wheels left dark stripes across the dusty floor.

We ran through the house examining everything. There was an old library full of cracked leather-bound books. There was a room with a billiards table. There was a big dining room with a table long enough to fit twenty guests.

Neither of us had seen anything like it. Most brownstones and apartments in New York are teeny weeny. But this house seemed to have huge amounts of space. It was magical! In all the excitement, I almost forgot the fact that we were going to have to leave New York in a week.

We ran up the stairs and looked at the second floor. There were several bedrooms and two bathrooms with very old, peculiar-looking fixtures. The ceilings were water-stained and the floors were grimy.

On the wall of one room was an ancient framed poster advertising a Broadway show called *Little Miss Cupcake*. There was a picture of a little girl dancing in a costume with big feathers sticking out of it. Despite the mildew and fading, I recognized it as the same little girl who was in the picture downstairs. The poster said, "Featuring Little Emma Rogers."

"Emma Rogers," Hana said. "Wasn't she like a big Broadway star a long time ago?"

"Oh, yeah," I said. "I remember Dad saying that this house used to belong to some actress."

We left the room and continued down the hall.

"Okay, this is getting creepy," I said as we entered the last of the six bedrooms. Something about it made me shiver.

The last bedroom was empty. No furniture or anything. I shined my flashlight around the room. In the corner was a small door. The door was big enough for me or Hana to get through, but it hardly seemed big enough for grown-ups. We opened it cautiously. Behind the door was a narrow, dark staircase.

"Where do you suppose it goes?" Hana said.

"This is kinda shiverlicious!" I said. "You think there are ghosts up there?"

"Zoism!" Hana said. We both laughed.

"You first," Hana said.

"No *you* first," I said.

We pushed and shoved and giggled and then finally I went up the narrow staircase. Hana trailed behind me.

When we got to the top floor, we found ourselves in a dark, cramped attic. Other than the beam of the flashlight, it was pitch black. For a moment, we froze.

"What's that sound?" Hana said.

There was a soft noise on the far side of the attic, a sort of *plop-plop-plop* sound. It was starting to be more *shiver* than *licious*!

I shined my light across the attic floor. To my relief, all I saw in the far corner was a small puddle. "Whew! It's just water," I said. Then I shined the light up toward the ceiling to see where it was coming from.

What I saw made us both gasp. Where there should have been a ceiling, there was instead a tangle of weird, black, snake-like things that twisted and dangled and mingled everywhere. My heart was like *gzzzzhhhh!* Right up in my throat!

Hana screamed.

When we stopped running, we were down at the bottom of the little staircase.

I slammed the door and leaned my back against it.

Hana sagged against me. "Oh my gosh!" she said, hugging me as though she didn't even have the strength to stand up. "What *was* that stuff?"

I shook my head. My heart was pounding and my palms were clammy. "I don't know. And I don't want to find out!"

Hana was trembling. For a moment we just stood there, trying to catch our breath.

"Let's go," I said finally.

But as we got to the door of the bedroom, Hana stopped and said, "Oh, no!"

"What?"

"I left my skateboard up there!"

I swallowed. I *so* didn't want to go back up there. With all that glistening black snaky-looking stuff? No way! For a moment, we just stood there. Suddenly we heard a thump.

Hana grabbed me again. "What was that?" she whispered.

My heart was racing. I strained to hear. "It sounds like it's in the hallway," I whispered.

Thump. Thump.

Whatever it was, it was coming right toward us.

Thump! Thump! Thump!

The only way to get away was to go back up the stairs into that creepy attic.

"I'm not going back up there," I said.

Suddenly the door to the bedroom flew open. Silhouetted in the door was a huge man with a monstrous, misshapen head. His arm was upraised, a giant stick in his hand.

"Aaaaggghhh!" he shouted and charged into the room.

We both screamed. I thought in that instant that I was about to die.

CHAPTER THREE

As the man charged into the room, he turned on a flashlight. The beam caught me and Hana, pinning us to the wall. We froze.

Suddenly the man stopped. He lowered the stick.

"Oh, for Pete's sake!" he said angrily. "You scared the bejeezus out of me!" Now that my eyes had adjusted, I saw that the man was a construction worker. What had looked to me like a huge, misshapen head was actually a yellow construction helmet. The man also wore a reflective orange vest printed with the words "Barrington Smith Construction Co."

Hana and I looked at each other. "How do you think *we* felt?" I said. "I thought you were some kind of monster!"

The man scowled. "Alright kids, get outta here. You know good and well you're not supposed to be playing in this house. This is very dangerous."

"But," Hana said, "my skateboard's up in the attic."

The man gestured at the door to the hallway with his stick. "Come on, girls, this isn't a safe place to play. Let's go. Now."

We dutifully trudged down the hallway and then down the stairs to the ground floor.

Several men stood in the living room. Two of them wore construction outfits like the big guy from upstairs. They both carried clipboards and rolled-up blueprints. The third man wore a beautiful suit. I stared. It was Barrington Smith himself.

He was shorter than he looked on TV, with pale, blotchy skin.

Barrington Smith stared at us. "Who are you?" he demanded.

"My name is —" I started.

"Do your parents know you're breaking into private property?" Barrington Smith interrupted. "This place is about to be demolished. Do you realize what would happen to you if you were inside here when this place got smashed?"

"Well —"

Again, Barrington Smith didn't seem interested in hearing my answers to his questions.

"Where do you two live?" he demanded.

"Um . . . across the street," I said. "But —"

"Ray!" Barrington Smith snapped his fingers at the big man in the orange vest. "Go over and tell these kids' parents that if I ever catch them in this place again, I'm filing a lawsuit against them."

"Yes, sir," the big man said. He motioned at the front door with his stick. "Go."

Two minutes later, the big man named Ray was knocking on the door of our house. I could smell his cologne, strong and fruity, as Mom answered the door. She had the same weary expression on her face that she'd had when she came home earlier that afternoon.

"Ma'am, is this your daughter?" Ray asked.

Mom squinted at him curiously. "Yes."

"Ma'am, my name is Ray D'Agostino with Barrington Smith Construction. We caught her and this other kid playing in that brownstone across the street. I've been instructed by Barrington Smith to inform you that if these girls trespass on that property again —"

Mom's face hardened. "Hold on, hold on!" she said. "What did you just say?"

"I said we found these two girls in that house over there." He pointed at the brick house across the street. The door was wide open. Inside I could still see the men with the clipboards and the blueprints. Barrington Smith was blabbing in a loud voice — I could hear it even across the street — and the two men were nodding and looking all serious.

Mom's mouth opened. "Am I seeing what I think I'm seeing?" she asked angrily.

"Ma'am —"

Mom shouldered her way past the construction worker and stalked across the street. Hana and I looked at each other, then scurried after her.

Mom walked up the steps to the front door of the old house and said, "What in the world do you people think you're doing?"

Barrington Smith turned and looked at her angrily. He was obviously not used to being talked to this way.

"Get out!" Mom shouted.

"Excuse me?" Barrington Smith finally seemed to have found his voice.

"Mr. Smith, you do not own this building. You will not own it for twenty-four hours. Until that time, your presence here is a violation of the law. Now get out of my building before I call the police and have you arrested for breaking and entering."

Barrington Smith eyed her for a moment. "So you're Jennifer Linden, huh? You've caused me an awful lot of trouble, you know that?"

Mom pointed at the street. "Out. Now."

The famous real estate developer jerked his head toward the door, signaling his men to leave. As he left, he smiled nastily. "In twenty-four hours

I'm flattening this crummy old wreck. And there's nothing you can do to stop me."

He pulled out a cell phone, made a quick call, and by the time he'd crossed the sidewalk, a black limousine was pulling up at the curb. A chauffeur hopped out and opened the rear door of the gleaming car.

"Love your outfit, doll," Barrington Smith said, winking at me. "See you around."

For a second I felt like, *Wow! Barrington Smith likes my crack-a-lacking fashion sense!* But then I was like, *What a jerk! Why do I care what he thinks?*

The chauffeur slammed the door shut and Barrington Smith was gone.

CHAPTER FOUR

When we got back to the house, Mom said, "Hana, you need to go home now."

Hana nodded and fled up the stairs to her apartment.

My mother opened the door to our apartment, her face still flushed with anger. "Zoe Nicole Linden," she said. "What were you doing in that building?"

"Um . . ." I tried to think of a good explanation. "Exploring?"

"Aside from the fact that the building is due to be blown up by Barrington Smith in about twenty-four hours, that house is very dangerous. It's old and it's falling apart. You could have been badly hurt."

I didn't know what to say. So I looked at the floor. I find it's best to get interested in the design on the carpet when somebody gets mad at you.

"How did you get in, Zoe?"

"I . . . uh . . . I borrowed the key off your thingy."

"What were you thinking!"

I shrugged and kept studying the carpet. "You said that if we lost that house, we couldn't afford to stay here, either," I said hopelessly. "I don't know. I just thought maybe —"

The anger slowly faded from Mom's face. "Look, this is a hard week," she said. "We're going to have to move next week. I'm not going to punish you. But just don't go in there, okay?"

Mom gave me a hug, then flopped down on the couch and stared at the ceiling.

"Can I ask you a question?" I said finally.

"Sure, baby," Mom said distractedly.

"We went up in the attic over there. It looked like the ceiling was covered with snakes or something. Do you know what that was?"

Mom frowned skeptically. "Snakes?" she said. Then her eyes widened and she grinned. "Oh! I know what you're talking about." She stood and walked to the window. "Come here."

I joined my mother at the window. Mom pointed at the old house. "See that tree up there?"

I could see the top of a tree peeping up over the roof of the brownstone. "Yeah, I was just saying to Hana that there aren't a lot of houses around here with backyards."

Mom shook her head. "There's no backyard."

"Then what —" I didn't get it. The tree had to be growing *somewhere*.

"That tree is actually growing out of the roof of the house. When your father and I bought the place, it had started growing around the chimney. We thought, *Oh, isn't that cute? A tree growing out of the roof.* Well, turns out, the root system has invaded the entire house. They're growing down the walls, inside the roof, down the drainpipes. It's caused all kinds of problems with the house. That's part of why I haven't been able to develop it."

"How can it do that?"

Mom shrugged. "It's actually drawing nutrients out of the plaster and the beams and the water pipes, I guess."

"But that's impossible."

Mom pointed at the tree. "Hey, there it is. You saw it growing in there."

I scratched my head. "That's totally cool. Weird, but cool."

"Yeah. When your dad and I bought it, we thought the same thing. Isn't that cool! But it turned out the roots have undermined the structure of the place. It was going to take a lot more money to fix it than we thought. Then once your dad died," she sighed. "I just didn't have the money or the energy to make it happen. Looking back, I should have sold out to Barrington Smith the minute he offered me a check. Instead, I kept fighting a losing battle."

"But he's going to ruin the neighborhood and put up some yucky apartment building."

Mom nodded sadly. I tried to think of something to say that would cheer her up. But I couldn't think of anything.

So we were going to be leaving my beloved New York in a week. It was almost too much to bear. I went over and got out my guitar and tried to play the new song I'd been writing. But I couldn't find any enthusiasm for it. It just seemed dumb.

So then I sang "New York, New York," that old song, in a loud, obnoxious, phony voice. I don't know why, but it made me feel a little better. Mom must have felt it, too, because suddenly we both totally cracked up. In fact, we laughed a lot longer than the actual funniness of it — if you see what I mean. Which is something I've noticed people sometimes do when they're a little bit sad.

"You know what?" Mom said when we both stopped laughing. "You're right."

I was puzzled. "Right about what?"

"If we're gonna leave New York, let's go out in a blaze of glory. No point in moping around."

"What do you mean?"

Mom stood up and clapped her hands together like she'd made up her mind about something. Then she walked over and opened a small wooden box that sat on the table by the door. Inside was a wad of green bills.

"This is all the money I have left," Mom said. "Let's just go blow it."

I stared at her.

"I'm serious!" Mom grinned. "Next week we're gonna be up in Utica living with Granny and Papa Jim, bored out of our skulls. So let's go out in style. Let's go to the best restaurant in Greenwich Village! Then we'll go up to Broadway and watch a show."

"You mean it?" I jumped up and down.

"Go get dressed. You better be looking *good*, too!"

I started to run to my room. Then I thought of something. I stopped. "Can Hana come, too?"

Mom smoothed out the wad of bills, counted them quickly. "Sure!" she said, grinning. "Why not? It's only money!"

CHAPTER FIVE

It took the three of us almost two hours to get dressed. We tried on dresses and shoes, laughing and joking and giggling as we held clothes up to one another and looked in the mirror and struck poses. Even Hana — whose idea of dressing up is anything other than blue jeans — got into it.

We had so much fun, I almost forgot how sad I was feeling.

When we were finally done, I looked in the mirror.

"Perfect!" Hana said.

"Perfect!" Mom said.

But I wasn't so sure. There was something missing. The blouse was perfect. The vintage skirt? Perfect. The boots? Perfect. But . . . I couldn't put my finger on it, but I had this vague sense of disappointment.

"Something's missing," I said. "I don't know what. But something's missing."

Mom looked at her watch. "Our reservation's

in fifteen minutes," she said. "We'd better go."

"Wait!" I said. "I know!"

"What?" Mom said.

"Mr. Park's place is on the way. We'll stop there. He'll know just what I need."

Hana nodded. "It's true," she said. "Mr. Park always knows."

Mom grinned. "All right then. Let's do it!"

As we walked out the door and headed toward the vintage clothes shop owned by my friend Mr. Park, I looked around. And suddenly I had this strong recollection of my dad.

Dad was born in Greenwich Village and lived here all his life. It was his absolutely favorite place.

He used to tell me, "Zo, you're lucky, you live in the coolest place in the world!"

He was an architect who specialized in restoring historical buildings, so whenever we walked through the neighborhood he would point out details of the buildings around us, explaining when they were made, who had lived in them, why they were beautiful.

He could talk about doorknobs and lintels and pediments and all this architecture stuff until my eyes glazed over. But even when I didn't really know what he was talking about, I loved listening to him. Because you could see in his eyes how much he loved everything he was talking about.

Enthusiasm is catching, you know what I mean? When he talked, I felt happy.

He explained to me that a long time ago, New York City was just a little town clustered at the base of Manhattan Island, and that most of what's now city was still covered with farms and woods. Back then, Greenwich Village was a farm town with its own street layout. When New York City got bigger and swallowed up the whole island, including Greenwich Village, the Village got to keep its own layout. This makes it really confusing for some people because the streets often turn at funny angles when you come from the areas surrounding the Village.

Most of the long avenues up and down New York City were made by plowing straight up the island, smashing over whatever was there before. But not Greenwich Village. It kept the same quaint layout that it had years ago. The same brownstones are still there today. There are no giant skyscrapers, no boring glass and steel buildings covering the area in shadows.

My father loved that about Greenwich Village. It was like a little town within a huge city. "You

can always see the sun here," he would say.

He told me that he wanted to spend his whole
life here, restoring old buildings, keeping the spirit
of the town alive. "Without these buildings and
these streets," he once told me, sweeping his hands
in an arc across Bleecker Street, "everything this
Village stands for would just dry up and blow
away."

"It's not just buildings, though," he said. "For
almost a century, the Village has been full of poets
and painters and actors. Exciting people. Smart
people. Fun people!"

He pointed up Hudson Street toward the huge skyscrapers in midtown. "The people who build those big, faceless buildings are always trying to knock down parts of the Village and build huge apartments and office complexes. People like Barrington Smith. We have to fight them, Zo."

"Why?" I asked.

"Because if this just becomes another glass canyon of fifty-story apartment buildings, all the artistic people will leave and this will just be like every place else in New York. No artists, no street performers, no fashion designers."

"Yeah, but why do developers want to tear up this neighborhood?"

"Simple, Zo," he said. "Money. There's only so much land in New York City. The higher you build, the more money you make. They look at all these nice little houses and they think, 'Hey, I could fire up my bulldozer, flatten a couple of these places, and make millions.'"

I can still remember the last time Dad and I walked around the neighborhood. He was pretty sick by then and his clothes were hanging off of him like his body was made out of coat hangers. But he smiled the whole time we walked, pointing out people he knew, buildings he'd worked on,

38

houses he'd restored, talking about the famous artist who'd lived here or the actor who'd lived there.

When we finally got back to our apartment, he looked across the street and said, "Wish I was going to be able to fix up the tree house." He pointed at the old brownstone. At that time I didn't know what he meant when he called it a "tree house." He sighed. "But I guess I never will."

It was the first time he'd ever really admitted to me just how sick he was.

He smiled at me sadly and said, "I hope you always love the Village like I do."

Then he gave me a hug, his arms as thin and fragile as bird wings.

"I will, Daddy," I said.

CHAPTER SIX

s we walked through the Village now, past the quaint old houses and the familiar restaurants and stores and galleries, I just kept thinking, *This is home! How can we leave?* The crowds of trendily dressed people, the Italian, Greek, and Japanese restaurants wafting odors from every corner of the earth—this was my *whole life!*

I can't leave, I thought. *I won't! I have to do something!* But what —?

After a few minutes, we found ourselves on Waverly Place. We crossed the street by a sign advertising the services of a fortune teller, Madame Claire. On the other side was Mr. Park's shop, a vintage clothing store called Twice Beautiful.

I pushed open the door. A tiny bell rang. I took a deep breath and smelled the air. There was something about the slightly musty scent of old clothes that made me feel happy. That smell promised a thousand different garments that could be arranged into a million amazing outfits.

"Hi, Mr. Park!" I called. The owner of the shop, Mr. Park, was a white-haired Korean man who had been running the shop here for almost fifty years. He wore a beautiful blue suit and a gold necktie, with cuff links and a spread-collared shirt. The store was stuffed with old clothes. Crazy-colored clothes from the seventies. Gold lamé dresses from the fifties. Go-go boots from the sixties. Huge feather-covered hats that must have been a hundred years old. It was a wonderland of strange and exciting clothes.

"Zoe!" Mr. Park said. "My goodness, you're looking even more fashionable than usual. What's the occasion?"

I shrugged.

"Zoe and I are moving," Mom said. "We're having a last little blowout before we go."

Mr. Park's eyebrows went up. "Moving! Why?"

I looked at Mom. Mom sighed. "Right before Zach got the diagnosis, we bought a building as a fixer-upper. We were going to restore it and sell it. But I ran into all kinds of problems. Structural issues, permitting, financing . . ." She started rattling on about all the junk that had gone wrong with the house. Finally she added, "Barrington

Smith wanted it for an apartment complex and he just wore me down. I just kept shoveling money into the project. But I finally just ran out of money."

"Barrington Smith," Mr. Park said, shaking his head. "He's going to ruin the whole neighborhood with that awful building."

Mom nodded glumly. "Tell me about it."

"Which brownstone is it?"

"The red brick one on the corner where our street hits Bleecker."

"Really!" Mr. Park said. "The house Emma Rogers used to live in?"

"How did you know?" I asked.

"Who *doesn't* know Emma Rogers?" Mr. Park said. "Emma Rogers was one of the most famous musical theater performers back in the 1920s. She was a child star, but she kept acting on Broadway well into the fifties."

"Yeah, Dad told me all about her," I said.

Mr. Park stepped back and studied me. "I love your look," he said. "But there's something missing." He held up a finger. "Don't move!"

Eyes twinkling, he disappeared into the back room. "See?" I said to Mom. "He always has exactly the right thing."

Moments later, Mr. Park reappeared with a small wooden box in his hand. He opened it, and inside lay a small silver locket in a bed of faded purple velvet. Mr. Park lifted the locket and put it around my neck. "There!" he said. "Perfect."

I looked at myself in the mirror. The teardrop-shaped locket lay against the skin at the hollow of my neck, my blond hair curling around it. Mr. Park was right. It *was* perfect. I felt so grown up.

"It's a very special necklace," Mr. Park said. "The reason I thought of it is because it was originally owned by Emma Rogers."

"Wow!" Hana said.

I turned around so Mom could see it, expecting to see her smile. Instead, she frowned.

"I'm sorry, Mr. Park," Mom said. "But I'm afraid we really can't afford it."

Mr. Park cocked his head and looked at her curiously. "It's a gift, my dear," he said.

Mom shook her head. "No, I'm sorry, but we can't accept it."

Mr. Park put one hand on my mother's arm. "I know how much you love this neighborhood," he said. "But what makes this place special is not the buildings. It's the people. Zoe has been coming into my shop ever since she was old enough to convince you to bring her here. Every time she visited, she brought a ray of sunshine into my day. You can't put a price on that, dear. She will be missed." He took my hand and placed it over the locket. "Keep it. And when you look at it, think about our little village."

"Please!" I said. "Please, Mom!"

"I won't take no for an answer," Mr. Park said.

Mom smiled at Mr. Park, then at me. "Okay. Since you put it that way."

"There's an interesting story about this box," he said. "As you can see, the box is much larger than the locket. According to the person who sold it to me, the box originally held a very valuable tiara. But the tiara was stolen. Apparently, it was quite a famous case back in the 1920s. Later, Emma Rogers put this locket in the box and then gave the box to a friend of hers."

My eyes widened. "I think we saw that tiara!" I said. "Her mom was wearing it in a picture that's hanging in the house."

"Too bad you didn't find the tiara itself," Mr. Park said. "I'd imagine it would be worth a mint."

Two hours later, after a fabulous dinner, we were getting off the subway at Times Square. Throngs of people poured out of the entrance onto 42nd Street. Times Square is like a huge canyon of lights. People from everywhere across the globe laughed and smiled and stared. I could hear them speaking Japanese, French, German, Spanish, and tons of other languages I couldn't even identify.

You might think this is weird, but even though I live in New York, I haven't been to Times Square very often, especially not at night. I gawked just like all the tourists. Even though it was already night, you wouldn't have known it standing there. There must have been millions of light bulbs

shining and flashing and blinking down on us!
Above us, giant television screens hung from
the tall buildings. Beautiful models lounged on
billboards hundreds of feet high. Theater signs
proclaimed the names of famous actors. Headlines
scrolled across giant signs.

"Look, there's the MTV studio!" Hana said.

"There's the Eisenberg Theater," Mom said.
"Did you know that Emma Rogers starred in the
first show there? *Little Miss Cupcake,* I think it
was."

I felt a grin break out on my face. "For the
worst day of my life," I said, "this sure is the best
day of my life!"

Mom smiled sadly and squeezed me to her
side. "Yeah," she said. "I know just what you
mean."

It was hard to believe, I thought, that in a week we'd be packing up our things and moving up to Granny and Papa Jim's house in Utica. Utica is a medium-size city in upstate New York. Nothing against Utica, but it's not exactly Excitement Central.

My grandparents live in a subdivision where all the houses look the same and all the people go to normal jobs at normal times of day and the strip malls look like the strip malls in every other town I've ever been to.

Not like New York City. Not like Greenwich Village.

Utica could never be home.

"Let's go see the show," Mom said.

I felt myself brighten. *The show!* For years I'd heard other kids talking about the show we were going to — about the wild costumes and the amazing dancers and the great songs. Now I was finally going!

The traffic light on 42nd Street turned green and the crowd surged forward. As I stepped into the street, I felt someone bump into me. I stumbled, then righted myself and continued across the street. But I couldn't help feeling that something wasn't right. It was only when I reached the other

side of the street and put my hand to my throat
that I realized what it was.

"My locket!" I screamed. "It's gone!"

CHAPTER SEVEN

When we got home, Mom handed me the empty jewelry box Mr. Park had given us.

"I'm sorry about the locket," Mom said.

I nodded glumly. I felt really tired suddenly. "I'm going to bed," I said.

I went back to my room, changed into my pajamas, and sat on my bed with the empty box on my lap. It was hard to believe that in less than a week we'd be moving.

I opened the box and looked inside. The old velvet still had the imprint of the tiara that it hadn't held for more than seventy-five years. And now the locket it had contained was stolen, too. Maybe the box was bad luck.

"Stupid box," I said, throwing it on the floor. When it hit the ground, the little frame holding the velvet popped out and something spilled out onto the floor next to the bed.

I frowned. What was it?

I leaned over and moved the box. Underneath

it — apparently hidden underneath the velvet all these years — was a very old envelope.

I picked it up and looked at it. It was addressed to someone named Ruth Bacon. The return address was written in faded ink. *Emma Rogers, 10004 Bleecker Street, New York, New York.*

I opened the flap, found a letter inside, and pulled it out. It read:

Dearest Ruth,

I wish you were here, as I am in quite a state. Something terrible has happened. Mother's tiara has been stolen!

I expect you might have heard about it. It's been in all the newspapers lately. While we were sleeping, a jewel thief climbed up on our roof and broke into the house through a window. I never even heard him. But I woke up in the middle of the night. I was freezing because the thief left a window open. Can you imagine! Some horrible person sneaking through your home at night?

The thief opened father's safe, and "made off into the night" as they say. I've been so afraid ever since.

*I hope you are doing better than I am
and that you are enjoying boarding school
and are not so lonely.
Your friend forever,
Emma
PS: I have a secret to tell you! But I have
to work up my nerve to tell you. Maybe I'll
tell you in my next letter.
PPS: It concerns mother's tiara.
PPPS: I know where it is!*

I sat up a little straighter. A secret! Secrets were always exciting. What could it be?

I picked up the box and shook it, wondering if there was a clue about where the tiara might be. Another letter, maybe?

But there was nothing else inside.

I put the box down on my bedside table, switched off the light, and lay down under the covers. I felt tired, but my mind just kept going around and around.

Suddenly I sat up, eyes wide. The tiara. *If I could find out what Emma Rogers knew, maybe I could find the tiara!* Mr. Park said it was worth a mint. If I could find it, we'd have lots of money. Then Mom wouldn't have to sell the house to

Barrington Smith. And we could afford to stay in New York City.

My hands started to shake. I was so excited.

And guess what? I didn't sleep all night. Not even for a *second!*

CHAPTER EIGHT

The problem with genius ideas you think of in the middle of the night is that they usually don't seem so genius the next morning.

When I sat down at the table and filled my bowl with Corn Flakes and said, "Hey, Mom, I'm going to find Emma Rogers's famous missing tiara and we'll be rich and we can stay in New York City," it just sounded silly.

"That's nice," Mom said, not looking up from the Saturday *New York Times*.

I read a book for awhile, then watched some Saturday morning cartoons, then picked up another book, then played on my computer. But I just kept thinking about the tiara, about how it would solve all our problems.

Finally, I got dressed and walked down to Mr. Park's shop. The bell tinkled as I walked in.

"Zoe!" he said. "How was your big evening?"

"It was pretty good," I said. "Except it was totally horrible."

Mr. Park tilted his head and looked at me curiously.

"Someone stole the locket," I said. "Right in the middle of Times Square. Just snatched it off my neck."

"Oh, sweetie, that's awful!"

"Yeah. But I found something interesting." I took out the letter and showed it to Mr. Park. He put his reading glasses on the end of his nose and read it.

"How mysterious!" he said, smiling.

I nodded. "So what I was wondering is, did they ever get the tiara back? Because if they didn't, wouldn't it be cool if we could find it?"

Mr. Park laughed. "That would be cool," he said.

"The problem is, there was only that one letter. Emma said she was going to tell her friend the big secret and explain what she knows about the tiara. But *that* letter wasn't in the box."

"How unfortunate," Mr. Park said. Then he frowned. "You know, I don't have any idea whether they ever found the tiara or not. I'm sure the person I got the locket from would know."

I felt a burst of excitement. "Where is she?"

Mr. Park's smile faded. "Well, unfortunately,

she died just last year." He shook his head sadly. "I bought the locket from Ruth Bacon, the girl that Emma sent this letter to. Only she wasn't a girl anymore, of course. Ruth and Emma both became actors, but Ruth didn't do quite as well as Emma did. She lived a very long time — and toward the end things got very hard for her. She had to sell off most of her possessions. She was over ninety years old." He looked thoughtful. "You know who you should talk to?"

CHAPTER NINE

For as long as I could remember, there had been a sign out on the sidewalk across the street from Mr. Park's shop that read, "Madame Claire FORTUNE TELLER." But I had never actually seen the fortune teller. I'd kept my eyes peeled for some gypsy-looking lady wearing a scarf and big hoop earrings and a peasant dress. But no luck.

So when Mr. Park led me through the door next to the sign and up the stairs, I was surprised. Madame Claire turned out to be this totally normal looking lady. She had very curly white hair and a round, pleasant face. No crystal ball either. She was typing at a computer in a very small room that looked like it could have been a dentist's office. When she saw us, her eyes crinkled like she was about to say something funny.

"Hi, Claire," Mr. Park said. "I have a visitor for you."

Madame Claire turned and looked at me. "You need your fortune told, honey?" she said. Her voice was low and smoky, and she had a strong Brooklyn accent. (Brooklyn is like Manhattan, one of the five parts, or "boroughs," of New York City.)

I blinked and didn't know what to say. I was thinking, like, *Where's the gypsy with the Dracula accent and the crystal ball?*

"Actually," Mr. Park said, "it's something else." Mr. Park turned to me and said, "Claire is kind of the unofficial historian of Greenwich Village. She might be able to answer the questions you have."

"Questions?" Madame Claire said. "What kind of questions do you have?"

I felt a little nervous. "Um, my mom owns the brownstone over on Bleecker Street that's about to be knocked down to make that apartment building."

"The old Emma Rogers place?" Madame Claire looked confused. "I thought Barrington Smith owned that place."

"Not yet," I said.

"Very interesting lady, Emma Rogers. What do you need to know?"

"Well, she had something stolen from her when she was about my age," I said. "A tiara. I wanted to find out if it was ever recovered."

Madame Claire's left eyebrow went up. "Have a seat, hon," she said, waving at a worn couch on the other side of the tiny room. Madame Claire looked thoughtfully up in the air. "Emma Rogers's father was a man named Billy C. Rogers. He started out as a singer and a dancer, then he bought a theater called The Heliotrope. It was quite successful and he made a lot of money at it. He married another singer by the name of Lucy Wilson. So Emma grew up around music and performers. They gave famous parties and people would come to their house and sing and play music and dance. It was a very exciting way to grow up, I'm sure.

"Anyway, somewhere along the way, Emma's father bought her mother a tiara. It made quite a big splash, because he paid an enormous amount of money for it. One day they threw a huge party. All the big performers and athletes of the day, and even some snooty rich people were there. Emma's mother wore the tiara, of course. When the party was over, according to what she told the police, she put it in the safe. The next day, it was gone."

"It was reported in the newspapers and there was a big investigation. Some people thought somebody at the party had probably done it. There were a lot of criminals involved in the theater business back then. Some people thought it was stolen by a jewel thief who broke into the house. Some people even thought that Mrs. Rogers herself stole it and filed a false claim for the insurance." Madame Claire shrugged. "But no one ever found out. The tiara was never recovered."

This was *totally* great news! I took out the letter I had found and passed it to Madame Claire. The fortune teller read it and then looked up at me. "Well, well!" she said. "So we have a mystery."

I nodded.

"So this letter was written to Ruth Bacon." Madame Claire looked thoughtful. "Ruth was a pretty well-known performer on Broadway, too. I think she —" She scratched her head. "I seem to remember that she donated her papers to some library. Hold on a second." She pecked away at the computer for a moment. "Yeah, here it is. She donated all her letters and her journals to the American Academy of the Theatrical and Performing Arts." She typed some more. "It's some kind of organization that, let's see, okay . . . yeah, their headquarters are over near New York University."

New York University was only a few blocks

away from where I lived!

"Thank you very much," I said. "This is a big help!"

"You're welcome," Madame Claire said. She studied me for a minute. "So what's troubling you?"

"I thought you were a fortune teller," I said, smiling. "Shouldn't you be able to tell me?" She seemed like the kind of person you could joke around with.

Madame Claire laughed. Then she pressed her eyes shut and put her fingers on her temples. "Let's see. . . You're about to lose your house. Your mom is broke. You're afraid you're going to have to move out of New York and go to . . . let me think! Wait! Wait! Ah . . . you're afraid you're going to have to move to Utica."

Whoa! I'd been making a joke, but it was like she read my mind! I gasped. I had always figured fortune telling was just some rip-off for tourists.

"Awesome! How did you know?"

Madame Claire winked. "Mr. Park told me yesterday," she said.

"Oh." I laughed sheepishly, feeling a little dopey.

Madame Claire's smile faded and she fixed her eyes on me. Honestly, it made me a little nervous. Finally she said, "Okay, here's my prediction. If that tiara can be found, you'll be the one to do it."

"Really?"

"If. . ." Madame Claire said gently, ". . .*if* it's there to be found."

CHAPTER TEN

I went back to my house and said to Mom, "Can I take a walk over near NYU?"

"What for?" Mom asked. She was sitting there at the table reading the paper, drinking coffee, still wearing her bathrobe and slippers.

"Nothing," I said. "I just want to take a walk."

"I'd rather you didn't go that far, but if you take Hana with you . . . ."

"Okay. Actually, you remember how I said I was going to find Emma Rogers's tiara?" I said. "So we wouldn't have to leave New York?"

She finally looked up, a distracted expression on her face. "Huh?"

I looked at Mom for a minute. This wasn't like her, sitting around in her bathrobe all day. "Are you giving up?" I said. "We can still keep our house if we find that tiara."

Mom gave me a sad smile and ruffled my hair. "Look, pumpkin, it's really sweet that you want to help. But there's nothing we can do now."

Then she looked back down at her paper.

"I'm going to go get Hana," I said.

"That's nice," Mom said.

Twenty minutes later, Hana and I were standing in front of a grimy old building near Washington Square Park. The front of the building was covered with all sorts of old stone carvings of strange looking faces and goofy masks. It looked sort of like the front of some ancient cathedral had been glued onto an American building. Next to the front door was a sign that said "American Academy of the Theatrical and Performing Arts. NO SOLICITING!"

We walked in and followed a set of wide marble stairs up to the second floor of the building. In front of us was an unmarked door.

I looked at Hana. She shrugged. I pushed

open the door and Hana followed me in. We found ourselves in a very large, echoing room with a vaulted ceiling. There were bookshelves lining all the walls, and glass cases here and there containing theatrical memorabilia: posters, costumes, musical instruments. In front of us was a very high, long desk that looked like it came from a library. A small, sour looking man sat at the desk reading. He wore a suit and a bow tie, and a few straggling strands of hair were pulled across his bald head. Otherwise there was no one in the place at all.

I felt a little weird, because this obviously wasn't a place where a lot of kids came. But I squared my shoulders and walked up to the desk. It was a very high desk, so high that I had to stand on my toes to see over the edge. The bald man didn't seem to notice I was there. I cleared my throat really loudly. The man didn't move. There was a bell on the desk. I reached up and banged it with my hand. A tiny *ting* echoed through the vast, empty room.

The man looked down irritably at me. He wore thick glasses that magnified his eyes, making him slightly creepy looking. "What?" he said sharply.

"Hi!" I said, trying not to sound too nervous.

"My name is Zoe Linden. I'm doing a project for school, and, um, I'm researching this lady, Emma Rogers. Emma Rogers, the actress?"

"I'm well aware of who she is."

"Yeah, okay. And I was told that her friend Ruth Bacon had donated some of Emma's stuff here?"

"*Stuff*?" The man stared unblinkingly at me.

My heart started beating fast. Did the guy have to be such a pahookie? "Like her papers? Her letters? Stuff like that? You know what I mean?"

The man grimaced. "No, actually, I *don't* know," he said.

"Her papers. They were donated here. I read it on the Internet."

He just kept looking at me with his huge eyes. "Oh," he said sarcastically, "the *Internet*. Well, then!"

Why was he being so mean? It seems like there are some grown-ups who just enjoy making kids feel bad. "I was wondering if I could look at them."

The man didn't answer. Instead, he indicated a worn sign on the desk, then nudged it about half a gajillionth of an inch toward me with one knuckle. The sign said, "Reference materials in our library available only to fully accredited research professionals."

Then he picked up his book and started reading again.

For a moment I felt like just running away. I felt like such a *kid*. But then I thought about how important this was. I just *had* to find out about that tiara. If I didn't, my life was over! I looked around the big room, trying to think of some way of finding the papers I needed to look through.

Next to the desk was an old card catalog, the kind libraries used to use back before they had computers. By the card catalog was a little display stand with a pair of cowboy boots, a cowboy hat, and a guitar that had been used by some Broadway star I'd never heard of.

Then I had an idea. *Geniosity!* I thought.

"We probably ought to go," Hana said.

I leaned over and whispered my idea to Hana.

"Are you sure?" Hana asked nervously.

"It's worth a try," I said. My heart was beating a million miles an hour. I took a deep breath, then I walked over to the display, picked up the guitar, and started tuning it.

The balding man jumped up like someone had shwoiked him in the head with a cattle prod. "You can't use that!" he shouted. "That used to belong to Newland Fellkirk!"

"I'm sure he won't mind," I said. "According to this sign, he's been dead a good while."

I twiddled with the E string, then strummed a chord. A little flat, but not too bad.

I began singing in a loud voice:

"Please, Mr. Academy of Thingamabob librarian,

Don't be such a mean . . . uh . . ."

I tried to think of a word that rhymed with librarian. Which is not easy, believe me!

". . . shmyhairyin!

I won't hurt Emma Rogers's papers or letters.

I just want to make my life betterers."

The man stared at me like I was some kind of gross bug that had just crawled up on his desk.

"I know this song and dance

Probably puts a wedgie in your pants.

But pleeeeeease give me

A chance!"

"Young lady, put that down this instant!" he shouted, jumping off the high stool that he was sitting on.

Meanwhile, Hana was frantically searching through the card catalog, flipping through all the cards that listed the books and papers the library had. I began retreating from the desk, trying to distract the bald guy so that he wouldn't notice what Hana was up to.

"Emma Rogers lost her tiara
And I'm hoping it didn't go far-ah!
So all I need to do
To tell . . ."

The man leapt at me, snatching at the guitar. I began to run, still thrashing away at the strings. (Which is not easy!) And the faster I ran, the faster I played. And the faster I played, the faster I sang.

"SoallIneedtodo. . .Totellyouthehonesttruth
Istakeaquickpeek . . .
AtheletterthatIseek . . .
Sowhybesuchameanie!"

I was running as fast as I could now, the librarian panting as he tried to keep up with me. By this point I had completely stopped worrying about the tune or the rhyme or whatever. I was just running and blabbing and hammering away at the same E chord. And then finally I couldn't think of anything to sing anymore.

I looked over at the card catalog and saw that Hana was gone. Yes! The first stage of my plan was a success.

"All right . . . young lady!" the librarian shouted. He was completely out of breath now. Apparently he didn't run very much. "You think . . . you're funny . . . " he gasped. "But . . . you won't be laughing . . . when I . . . call the . . . police."

I stopped running and walked back toward the display where the guitar came from. I was not real psyched about the idea of getting grabbed by the police. Plus, I could see Hana up on the second floor balcony, standing on a ladder and pulling something off a shelf. If I could just distract Mr. Baldy for a few more minutes.

"Okay, okay, okay!" I said, setting the guitar down. "You win. I was just hoping that maybe you'd be nice and help a kid out." I walked over toward the door and started waving my arms as I talked, rolling my eyes and making all these goofy faces. Anything to distract the man from what Hana was doing. I mean, it wasn't like he could call the police on me for making faces. "I can see you're not going to help, though, sir. I can see you're just way too *busy* and *important* to help out a mere kid such as myself."

Up on the second floor, Hana was climbing down the ladder.

"I'm sorry we caused you any trouble," I said.

I kept waving my arms and making faces. "Have a great day. Have a great life. Have a . . . a . . . a . . ." I couldn't think of anything else to say.

Fortunately, Hana appeared at just that moment.

"We were just leaving," Hana called out.

I waved as Hana pulled me out the door.

We pounded down the steps and out the front door, laughing. Out on the street, we kept running until we couldn't run anymore.

"Oh, my gosh!" Hana said. "Zoe, that was the funniest thing I've ever heard. That was the worst song *ever!*"

I was laughing so hard now that my sides were aching. Hana leaned against the wall of one of the New York University buildings, cracking up until tears started streaming down her face. "That was total genius!"

"I know!" I said. Then we fell on the ground laughing.

"So," I said when we finally stopped laughing. "Did you find the letter?"

Hana's smile faded. She cleared her throat and looked at the ground. "Actually, no. It wasn't there."

CHAPTER ELEVEN

I t wasn't there?" I said desperately. "So they didn't have it?"

"Well. . ." Hana frowned. "They did . . . but they didn't."

I cocked my head. "Huh?"

Hana shrugged. "Well, it said in the card catalog that they had a bunch of letters from Emma Rogers to Ruth Bacon. They gave a number for the file thingy that it was supposed to be in. So I went to where the file was and took it down. But it was totally empty."

"Totally?"

"Well, except for this."

She pulled out a piece of red paper that had been folded in half. When she unfolded it, I saw it said, "These Documents on Loan."

"To who?" I wondered out loud. "Who were they loaned to?"

Hana's eyes widened. She handed the paper to me.

"These documents on loan," I read, a wave of frustration washing over me, "to the Barrington Smith Historical Foundation. That sounds totally bogus."

"What would Barrington Smith want with those letters?" Hana said.

I wondered the same thing. "I don't know," I said angrily. "But I think we need to find out!"

As we were walking home, a group of high school boys ran by us, laughing and talking in loud voices. There was something I smelled as they walked by that triggered a memory.

"Oh, my gosh!" I said.

"What?" Hana said.

"Cologne," I said softly.

Hana looked at me like I'd just lost my mind. "So? What about it?"

"Did you smell that boy's cologne?" I asked.

Hana waved her hand in front of her nose. "Smelled like he fell into the bottle."

"Did you recognize it, though?"

Hana looked puzzled. "What do you mean?"

"The guy at the house the other day," I said. "The big guy in the construction hat? Ray D'Agostino or whatever his name was? He wore that same cologne."

"So?"

I leaned toward Hana. "I smelled that same cologne when my locket got stolen!"

"You think he's the one who stole it?"

I thought about it for awhile as we walked home. We reached the corner of Bleecker and Grove Streets, along the back of my Mom's tree house. "Oh my gosh," I said.

Three houses had already been torn down, leaving an ugly bare patch of ground. In the middle of the bare ground was a small trailer, sort of like a mobile home. It was jacked up on concrete blocks. On the side of the trailer hung a large sign: Barrington Smith Construction, Ray D'Agostino, Construction Supervisor.

We stared at the ugly little trailer. So it was already happening. Barrington Smith was already starting his project to ruin the neighborhood.

There was a fence around the property, but it was unfinished. It looked like they had been working on the fence on Friday afternoon, then quit for the weekend. Since today was Saturday, though, no one was working at the construction site. So there was nothing to stop someone from strolling right up to the trailer.

"Maybe we could get two things done at once!"

Hana said with a smile.

I grinned back at Hana. "Maybe we could!"

We didn't say what we had in mind. But we both knew. Hana and I are like that — we just know what the other person is thinking without even having to say it.

We looked both ways, up and down the street. A few people were walking by, but no one wearing hard hats. In New York, no one pays attention to what anybody else is doing. So as long as the Barrington Smith Construction guys weren't there, I wasn't worried about getting in trouble.

"Let's go!" I whispered.

We trotted across the empty lot as quickly as possible. There was a musty smell, like old basements. We ran up to the door of the trailer.

"Here, I'll knock," Hana said. "Then let's hide and see if anybody's here."

She rapped on the door *pow pow pow*. Then

we ran off and hid behind a rusty barrel full of trash. I waited a second, then peeped out. Nobody had answered the door.

"I think it's safe," I whispered. We stood up and approached the little trailer again. I tried the handle, but it was locked.

"Hmm," Hana said. "That's a problem. I don't suppose you know how to pick locks, huh?"

"Well, I read this book once that explained the theory." Then she laughed. "Uh, so the answer is no."

I laughed too, then leaned over and looked under the trailer. It was kind of spooky underneath there. Dark, dirty—and with that basement smell.

I was wearing my fourth-favorite pair of jeans and really didn't want to get them dirty. But still, I knew that my future depended on being able to find the tiara. "What the heck," I said. Then I got down on my knees and started crawling underneath the trailer.

"What are you looking for?" Hana asked.

"I'll know when I see it," I said. My voice sounded all flubby and squashed underneath the trailer.

I kept crawling along. Above me was a bunch

of dirty insulation and wires and metal bars and stuff. Suddenly I bumped my head.

"Ow!" I said.

"You okay?" Hana called.

It was so dark where I was that I couldn't really make out what I'd bumped into. I felt it with my hand. It was a flat, swingy thing, cool to the touch. Like some kind of metal door.

Wait a sec! A *door?*

I pushed on it a little. It swung on hinges. It *was* some kind of door!

I pulled myself a little farther with my elbows, until I could look straight up.

It was a very small door. Not like a people door; more like a dog door. Or maybe it was for heating vents to go through or something. I didn't really care. I figured I'd try to crawl through it. The door was way too small for a grown-up to get through, so maybe that's why they didn't worry about locking it.

I poked my head through. I could see a very dark, junky looking room with cheap paneled walls and a cheap metal desk over in one corner. An old, battered computer sat on the desk. I put one arm through the hole and started forcing my way up through the little door in the floor. It was pretty snug, and for a second I had this giant panic attack, thinking I was going to get stuck. My heart started going *gunk gunk gunk gunk* in my chest. But then I was like, *Hey, calm down, Zo!*

I took a couple of deep breaths, then just jammed myself straight up. I could hear the metal sides of the door scratching their way across my clothes.

And then I was in!

I hopped up, ran to the door, opened it, and let Hana in.

"You look over there," I said, pointing at the desk, "and I'll look over here in this filing cabinet. Maybe either the letter or the locket will be here."

I opened the top drawer of a gray metal filing cabinet while Hana started rummaging through the desk.

There were some files in the cabinet. I didn't really understand what they were for. Each file was labeled—payroll, insurance, workers' comp, permits, OSHA—it was all boring grown-up stuff that didn't mean anything to me. I looked through each folder as quickly as I could, hoping to find some crumbly old letters. But no luck.

I closed the top drawer, moved on to the next. More boring papers.

"We better hurry," Hana said as I flipped through the second drawer. "You never know, they might have some kind of alarm in here."

I hadn't thought of that. I slammed the second drawer shut. One drawer left.

I pulled it open. It was dead empty.

"Darn it!" I said, looking over at Hana.

She looked up at me and shook her head. "Nothing."

"Oh, well," I said. "Nothing ventured, nothing gained."

"What about the computer?" Hana said.

I shrugged. "Couldn't hurt."

Hana thumbed the button on the front. It hummed to life. We stared at the screen until it asked us for a password.

"Oh, well," I said. I'm not that great with computers.

But Hana just typed in some stuff and then hit the enter key. *Welcome Ray D'Agostino,* the screen said.

"How'd you *do* that?" I asked.

"Pure genius," she said. Then she grinned and opened the top drawer of the desk. Somebody had written *Password: 22157* on the bottom of the drawer in black marker.

"Oh," I said. "I never would have thought of that."

"Everybody keeps their password in their desk," Hana said, using the tone of voice she always has when she talks to me about computers. "Didn't you know that?"

"What are we looking for?" I asked.

Hana shrugged. "Who knows?" She started clicking the mouse. "Maybe his e-mail?"

She clicked on his e-mail folder and found all of Ray's outgoing mail. Most of the e-mails were about construction stuff. Snoozoriously boring! We kept scrolling through the letters.

"Wait!" I said pointing at the screen. "Check that one. It's to Barrington Smith himself."

We read the e-mail.

> *Mr. Smith,*
>
> *I got those items we were talking about from the academy. I told them I was with the Barrington Smith Historical Foundation. Which I thought was kind of a nice touch, huh? Anyway, what do you want me to do with the items?*
>
> *Ray*

The answer came back from Barrington
Smith: *Scan them, send me the scans, then burn the
originals.*

"Okay, now try this one!" I said.

There was an attachment on the next e-mail.
Hana clicked on it and an image appeared on the
screen. An image of a very old letter.

> *Dearest Ruth,*
>
> *I've finally worked up the courage to tell
> you what happened. Remember I was telling
> you about the night that the tiara was stolen?
> Well . . . it wasn't really stolen at all.*

Everybody was up really late, making all this noise at the party my parents were having, so I didn't sleep very well. Finally, at about two o'clock in the morning it got quiet. But by then I couldn't sleep. So I went downstairs to get a drink of water.

I had to go through father's study to get the water, whereupon I noticed that his safe was open. I looked inside and there was the tiara. I think probably it was very late when he went to bed and he was tired and forgot to close it. Anyway, I decided to take it out and put it on my head while I was getting my drink of water. I just love that tiara!

Then, I went back to bed. You might find it strange, but I had completely forgotten I was wearing the tiara.

Well, the next morning I awoke and found the tiara in my bed. I ran back into Father's study to put it back in the safe. Only my father had already closed it! I suppose he didn't even notice among all the other things in the safe that the tiara was gone.

What was I going to do? If I told my parents that I had taken it, they would have been very angry. So I decided I would hide it until an opportunity arose to figure out the combination. Father is terribly forgetful, so I knew he had written the combination to the safe on a piece of paper and left it in his desk. It was just a question of waiting until he was out of the house and then finding it.

I have a little secret place in my wall where I've been hiding certain items since I was little. So I pulled it open and inserted the tiara. Then I went out to play with Clara from next door.

When I got back, the house was full of policemen!

Evidently Mother had wished to check on the tiara, as one of the diamonds had come loose during the party. Father opened the safe and the tiara was gone. I needn't tell you that Father and Mother had a fit!

They immediately called the police. So there they were as I walked back into the house, telling this formidable looking detective about how the tiara had been stolen.

Of course, I ran up to my room to get the tiara.

Only, when I stuck my hand into my secret hole in the wall, the tiara was gone!

I didn't know what to do. I knew that

if I told them that I had taken out the tiara, they would be terribly upset — especially as it was now mysteriously gone again. I couldn't imagine what had happened. Was it possible that one of the servants had seen me taking the tiara into my bedroom and then snuck in and stole it after I left?

I was in an absolute tizzy!

I should have gone down and told them, of course. But I was too scared.

So I said nothing. Imagine, to my horror, that the next day the missing tiara was front page news. Father offered a reward, and Mother was crying, and everyone in the city seemed to have an opinion as to who stole it and why and how.

I can't sleep. I can't eat. I can't even read or sing or play the piano. I just lie around feeling sick all day.

With each day that goes by, I know that I'll be punished worse if I tell what happened. Could I be sent to jail? I'm in such a terrible fix. I wish you were here to help me!

Your best friend,
Emma

PS: If you want the truth, I think I even know where it is! I think it must have slipped down inside the wall. There's a sort of ledge inside my secret hole. If it fell off the ledge, it would just disappear into the darkness somewhere down inside the wall. I think the tiara is only inches away from me as I sit and write this letter. But I can't get it out of the wall without practically tearing up the entire room. And even if I do, then what? I'll get in such trouble! Oh, Ruth, what am I going to do? Please write soon!

There was one more attachment, another letter. It read:

> *Dearest Ruth,*
>
> *Thank you for your wise counsel. I think you are right. Father says the insurance company is going to pay him for it. So he's getting the money back anyway. I'm just going to leave it there.*
>
> *I know I've done a terrible thing. But I am resolved to put it behind me and forget it all together.*

Whatever happens, we will always have this secret. You must swear to never, never, never, never tell.

    Your dearest and best friend,
    Emma

"Whoa!" Hana said. "You think it's still there?"

"I think Barrington Smith must think it's there. Otherwise, why did he go to all this trouble?"

Hana nodded.

"We're gonna be rich!" I said.

"All we have to do is go figure out where it is!"

"Let's go!" I said.

But as we turned to the door, a loud voice said, "You're not going *anywhere!*"

CHAPTER TWELVE

Standing in the door was the big construction supervisor, Ray D'Agostino.

"Your mom may still own that house over there for another couple of hours," he said, "but she don't own *this* place."

I nudged Hana secretly and pointed at the trap door in the floor. Hana's thinner than I am, so I figured she could make it down the hole faster than I could.

She swallowed.

"Go!" I whispered.

"I'm calling the cops," he said. "See how your mom likes that, huh."

Hana made a break for the trap door. She stood over the hole for a moment, then jumped and *floop!* she was gone.

"Oh, no you don't!" Ray shouted. He scrambled toward the trap door, cutting me off. For such a big guy, he moved pretty fast. I could smell his cologne filling the little trailer now.

What he didn't consider, though, was that he couldn't guard both the door and the hole in the floor. I dove toward the door, then pounded down the concrete steps and into the yard.

"Hey!" he shouted.

I knew he was faster than me, so just running wasn't going to be enough. But I could see a small gap in the fence. If I could make it . . .

I saw Hana pop out from under the trailer. "You go that way!" I shouted, pointing in the opposite direction. Then I sprinted as fast as I could for the gap in the fence.

I could hear Ray pounding after me, grunting with every stride. Was I going to make it?

"Look out, Zoe!" Hana screamed.

I blasted the last ten feet to the fence and squeezed through the gap — just as a big meaty hand clamped down on my shirt. I struggled, but Ray was way too strong for me. He couldn't get through the gap in the fence, though.

"Why'd you steal the locket?" I said. "What was in there?"

"Huh?" he said angrily. "What are you talking about?"

"The locket. There's something in it, isn't there? A clue to where the tiara is."

The construction supervisor glared at me. "Don't think you're gonna distract me, sweetie pie," he said. With his free hand he pulled out a cell phone and dialed a number.

"Yeah, it's Ray," he said. "I caught them same two girls that was in the house over on Bleecker Street. No, not in the house. They broke into the trailer on the job site." He paused. "No, sir. No, sir, I'm not sure what they were doing. It seemed like they were looking at my e-mail. Uh-huh. Yes, sir. Uh-huh. It could have been those papers I scanned for you."

"I'm going to start screaming if you don't leave me alone!" I said.

"Mr. Smith, let's be realistic," Ray said. "I can't exactly kidnap them so we can find out." The way he was talking, I got the sense he didn't like Barrington Smith all that much. But that didn't make me feel much better as long as he had his hand clamped on my shirt.

"Look, I gotta go, Mr. Smith," Ray said. "The girl's kicking up a fuss."

He let go of my shirt.

Ray pointed his thick finger at me. "This isn't right, kid!" he said. "You can't just go breaking into places."

I saw Hana waiting for me at the corner.

"Yeah, well, you can't go stealing things from libraries," I said. "Love to chat, but I have to run."

And that's exactly what I did!

CHAPTER THIRTEEN

W e've got to get back in the house and look in that room," Hana said as soon as I caught up with her.

I nodded. "Yeah, that tiara's totally got to be in there!"

"But how do we get it out of the wall?" she asked.

"I've still got all of Daddy's tools," I said.

One year for Christmas my mom gave my father a set of custom-made tools from England. They all had beautiful wooden handles and brass fittings. As an architect, Daddy's job was to plan and direct the work on the buildings he restored. He didn't actually have to work on them himself. But he liked carpentry, so when he had spare time, he'd go over to one of the houses he was restoring and work with the carpenters.

And he always brought the tools Mom gave him. I think they were his proudest possession. They were neatly stored in a wooden box, each

hammer and saw and chisel with its own place. A small brass plate on the top said *Zachary T. Linden.*

The key to the building was still sitting on the table by the door. I palmed it as I walked past my mother. She was still sitting there reading the paper. I think she was really sad. Usually she's busy all day, never sits around. But today I don't think she felt like doing anything.

Two minutes later, Hana and I were nervously tiptoeing into the house again. Inside, it was very silent and dark. The windows were very dusty, making the sunlight seem weak and pale as it fell on the rotting carpets and sagging furniture.

"Woooooooooooo!" Hana made a ghost noise.

I laughed. But even so, it made my skin prickle. For some reason, I felt more scared as we climbed the stairs than I had the last time we were here.

"Which one do you think is hers?" Hana asked, meaning Emma's room.

"I don't know," I said. "She probably had one room when she was a kid and then moved to another one after her parents died and she took over the house. But maybe not."

We found a room with slightly newer furniture than the others. It had a couple of pictures of Emma Rogers on the wall looking all glamorous. "I bet this is it," Hana said.

"Yeah, but maybe this is her grown-up room," I said. "She might have lived in another room when she was a kid."

We kept checking the rooms. We'd been through them before, but then we weren't really looking for her room specifically that time. I didn't remember a roomful of kid's stuff, though. After looking at what seemed to be spare bedrooms, we entered the office. It had paneled walls and lots of books and a dusty deer head hanging on the wall. It looked like it had been decorated by a man, not a woman.

"Wonder where the safe is." I said.

"I bet it's behind that picture," Hana said. A painting of an old sailing ship hung on the wall by the deer. I pulled the picture down — man, was it heavy! — and leaned it on the floor.

"Ooo, *gross*!" Hana said.

There may have been a safe there once, but now, sticking out of a rectangular space on the wall, there was just a giant glistening knot of roots. It was just like Mom said, the roots of the tree on the roof had invaded the walls of the house.

We hurried to the last room on the hallway, the empty one with the stairs leading up to the attic.

"I bet this was it," Hana said. "I bet she moved out and cleaned it up after she grew up."

We stood there in the middle of the room.

"So . . . uh . . . how would we know where her secret hiding place was?" Hana said.

"Well, she said it was in the wall, right?"

Hana nodded.

"So she must have cut some plaster out." I walked over and put my hand against the wall. "Daddy used to show me houses when he was fixing them up. Houses this old have plaster that's glopped on over these wooden strips. It would make a big mess to cut a hole in it, so she would have had to put it somewhere that nobody would see it. Otherwise her parents would have been so mad at her!"

Hana laughed. "Yeah, but I don't see any holes anywhere."

We shined our flashlights around the room.

The walls were cracked, water-stained, and peeling. But there weren't any obvious holes.

"Wait a minute!" Hana said. "Go down to the far end of the wall and shine your flashlight along the wall. Right about this high." She held her hand a foot off the ground.

"Okay," I said, squatting on the floor. She turned her flashlight off as I shined mine along the wall. "What are we looking for?" I asked.

She stared carefully at the wall, then shook her head. "Let's try that wall." She pointed at the other side of the room.

"Yeah, but —" I didn't quite follow what she was up to.

"Right there," she said, showing me where she wanted me to shine the light.

I squatted down again. "Yuck!" I said. "It sure is dirty. My pants are gonna —"

"Hah!" she said.

"What?"

"Look!" There on the wall, a foot off the ground, was a shadow. A small, rectangular shadow no bigger than the palm of my hand.

I frowned for a minute, trying to see what the big deal was. Then I grinned.

"Total geniosity, Hana!" I said.

"She must have cut the hole when she was a kid. Then later on, she just plastered over it again. But you can see where it is because it sticks out. But only a teeny tiny bit." Hana tapped the wall. "The only way to see it is —"

"To shine the flashlight down the wall!"

I opened Daddy's box of tools, took out the hammer and pulled it back, ready to whack a hole in the wall. Then I hesitated.

"What are you waiting for?" Hana said.

"I don't know," I said. "I feel a little weird just shiracking a hole in the wall."

"Shiracking?" she said. "Is that a Zoism? Or have I just never heard it before?"

"I don't know," I said.

"Look, if we don't find this thing," Hana said, "Barrington Smith's gonna be bulldozing this place anyway."

"You make a good point," I said. Then I smashed the hammer into the wall.

The plaster gave way easily, and with two or three more whacks, a nice hole opened up.

"Look!" Hana said, reaching into the hole.

My heart leapt. "Did you find it?"

"No," she said. "But this must be her little hidey hole. See?"

She pulled her fist out then uncurled her fingers. Sitting in the middle of her palm was a tiny mouse made out of felt. It had googly little felt eyes and a little felt tail.

"Ohhhh!" I said, stroking it with my finger. "It's so cute!"

She stuck her hand in again and felt around. "There's a sort of ledge thing here, like she said in the letter. If the tiara fell off, it's going to be deeper in the hole. You'll need to knock out more plaster."

I banged the hammer on the wall a couple more times.

"Don't kill it!" Hana said. "If it's in there, you don't want to smash it."

I laughed. "Yeah that would be kind of a bummer if we found it and I'd smashed it to bits, huh?"

I hit the wall more gently. The problem was that the wood strips behind the plaster were really strong and didn't want to break. So the plaster cracked but didn't come apart.

Hana reached into the toolbox and came out with a pry bar. "Let's try this," she said.

She inserted the thin end of the bar into the wall, then yanked on it. The wood gave way and she fell backward onto the floor. "Oops!" she said.

"Oh no!" I said.

"What?" Hana said.

"You got shmutz all over your clothes!"

Hana made a face. "Yeah, like I care," she said, grinning as she dusted off the seat of her jeans.

I took the pry bar and yanked on it a couple more times, the wood splintering with each pull. It was kind of fun, actually, tearing up a house. We both got into it, ripping and tearing at the wall, until finally there was a giant hole that went all the way down to the floor.

"I can't see *anything*," I said, waving at the

cloud of white plaster dust.

Hana started coughing. "I think I'm gonna be sick."

We stepped back and let the cloud clear. After a minute, we shined our flashlights at the hole.

Hana groaned.

"Oh *no!*" I said.

The hole in the wall was empty. Totally, totally, totally empty.

"Could it have fallen deeper into the wall?" Hana said. "Maybe it fell down to the first floor."

I walked back to where we had been working and ran my hand across the dusty bottom of the hole. A heavy piece of wood covered the entire bottom of the hole. "Nope," I said. "This is called a stringer. They run along the inside of the wall on every floor. I don't think the tiara could have fallen past the stringer."

"Then, where is it?" Hana's voice was anguished. Usually she's so calm and logical. But suddenly it was like it had finally hit her that I was really leaving. "We have to find it! You can't leave New York. You *can't!*"

I felt completely defeated. "I know," I said softly. "But it's just not here."

Hana grabbed the hammer and started

smashing big chunks out of the wall. Plaster was flying everywhere.

"Hana," I said. "It's just not there."

But she kept whacking away like she was possessed. When she was done, the entire lower section of the wall was massacred. But there wasn't a tiara anywhere.

She turned back to me, her face all covered with white plaster dust. She looked like a ghost—except for the black streaks where her tears had washed away the plaster dust. She stood there for a minute, tears running down her face.

"I don't want you to go!" she wailed.

And then I was crying, too. We grabbed hold of each other and stood there bawling like a couple of babies.

Suddenly she straightened up and pushed me away. "This is dumb," she said, her voice quavering. "I'm supposed to be the calm one. You're supposed to be the one crying and everything."

Then we laughed sadly and sat down on the floor with our backs against the far wall, looking at the hole gaping from the plaster. I didn't even care that I was getting crud all over my fourth favorite pair of jeans.

I don't know how long we sat there, but it seemed like a long time.

"Where could it have gone?" I said.

Hana smacked herself in the forehead with the palms of both hands. "Think!" she said. "Think, think, think!"

"Probably when she grew up, she reached in there and got it out," I said. "Heck, she might have sold the stupid thing a gajillion years ago."

"Yeah," Hana said. "Yeah, that's probably right."

As if we had the same thought at the exact same moment, we both stood up and shuffled down the stairs. I felt numb now. The toolbox felt like it weighed about fifty tons. It whacked against my leg with every step.

So that was it. We'd tried. We'd failed. I was leaving New York.

End of story.

We walked out of the house. The light outside was so bright, I could hardly see. I turned back to the door, put the key in the lock and twisted it.

"Um . . . Zoe?" Hana said.

"What?" I said.

"Um, Zoe, I think we need to —"

"Run?" a voice said.

I turned and saw two men standing next to the stoop. One was tall and thin. The other was short and stocky. Stocky but not fat.

"Nah," the stocky man said, "I think it's a little late for running."

The tall guy reached up and grabbed the box of tools from my hand. "Thanks," he said. "I'll just take that."

Before I could even blink, the two men had climbed into a big black car that was idling at the curb and sped away.

"What just happened there?" Hana said.

"Daddy's tools!" I howled. "They took Daddy's tools!"

There was a long silence.

"Yeah," Hana said. "But, like, *why*?"

I watched the red taillights of the car recede down the street. I felt like somebody had punched me in the stomach.

"They must have figured we found the tiara and put it in the toolbox," I said. Then I started running after the car.

I don't know why I thought I'd catch up with the car. The best sprinter in the world can't catch a car. And I'm not in any danger of ever being the world's best sprinter. But I couldn't bear the idea of losing Daddy's tools.

"Zoe, wait!" Hana called.

But I just kept running.

At the end of the street, the big, black car stopped, cut off by a garbage truck. For a minute I got closer. I don't know what I thought I was going to do if I caught up with them. But I just had to keep going. I felt like the memory of my father was slipping away with every second that went by.

Just as I got within twenty or thirty feet of the car, the garbage truck moved and the black car surged ahead.

"Zoe!" I could hear Hana's footsteps behind me.

The black car crossed Bedford Street and tore down the road. I ran and ran, but the distance between us was getting bigger by the second. People on the street were staring at me. I guess I was screaming something at the men in the car, but I was so worked up I don't even know what I was saying.

Then, at Houston Street, the car took a sudden right turn. I saw something fly out the window.

Daddy's tools! They'd thrown the box out the window. They must have searched through it and realized the tiara wasn't there.

I skidded to a halt. Daddy's beloved tools had smashed into the curb in front of an Indian restaurant. People were seated at tables set out on the sidewalk, looking at me curiously. The box had shattered and the beautiful tools lay scattered across the rough concrete.

"Help me!" I called to Hana.

Hana ran up beside me, breathing hard. I fell to my knees and started grabbing wrenches and screwdrivers. Hana tried to fix the box, but it was completely wrecked. I piled the tools in a jumble.

I kept circling and circling, wider and wider circles, trying to make sure I didn't miss a single tool. The idea that even one of Daddy's precious tools might be missing was like a stab in my heart. I had to find them all.

Finally I was satisfied that I'd gotten every single one of them. I piled them carefully back into the wreckage of the box.

One of the waiters came out of the restaurant and held out a paper bag. "Here," he said. "Why don't you put those in here."

"Thanks," I said.

I set the bag on one of the empty tables outside the restaurant. Then Hana and I silently filled it with the tools.

When I was done, I said, "Well, so I guess that's it, huh?"

Hana had a funny look on her face. "Uh," she said. "Maybe not."

I frowned. "What do you mean?"

For a minute, she didn't speak.

"What?" I said.

When she finally spoke, it was just one word. "Run!"

I turned and looked behind me. A black car was screeching to a halt. Before it had stopped, the two men who'd taken the tools were climbing out.

"I'll distract them!" Hana said. "Just run."

"But . . . Daddy's tools!" I said.

"They don't care about the tools," Hana said, scooping them up into her arms.

The bigger of the two men was striding toward me. "Where is it?" he yelled.

"Hey," the waiter said. "You guys need to leave these girls alone."

The big man didn't even slow down. He plowed right over the waiter, who fell in a heap.

"Run!" Hana said again.

The expression on the big man's face scared me to death. So I did what Hana said.

I ran.

CHAPTER FOURTEEN

I couldn't tell you exactly where I ran. I ran through alleys and hid behind dumpsters. I ran behind buildings and crawled under fences. The two men were faster than me. They were grown-ups. They were probably in good shape.

But I knew every inch of the Village. I knew where you could hide and where you could run, where cars could go and where they couldn't.

So I managed to stay ahead of the men.

But they kept coming. I kept trying to circle around and get back home. But I couldn't seem to get there. Eventually I ended up in the Meatpacking District, the area where they used to slaughter animals. It's a kind of spooky area, full of old warehouses and slaughterhouses, slowly being pushed out by trendy restaurants and even trendier designer stores. The restaurants are open late, but the area with the real meatpacking plants is busy early in the morning and is mostly deserted later in the day. The streets are old cobblestone. Sometimes you could almost think you're in the New York of 100 years ago.

If I'd only run in the other direction, I'd have been in an area full of people. But the area where I had gotten myself just didn't have many people on the street. So I started working my way north and back east again. Back in the direction I'd come. And the two men kept getting closer and closer.

Suddenly, I thought I'd caught a break. I was getting close to home—West 10th Street, the street that parallels Christopher Street, where I live. I saw the construction site where the trailer was. I remembered that there's a little alleyway that runs through the back of the construction site and over to Christopher Street.

If I could make it to that, I'd practically be home.

I ducked through the gap in the fence that I'd used to escape from Ray D'Agostino and headed toward the alley. The two men were too big to make it through the gap, so they had to run around it. I could hear their footsteps behind me. My lungs were burning and my legs felt like rubber.

I saw a scrap of sunlight coming at me through a gap between the buildings. It was the alley! I'd made it.

Then I looked down and my heart sank. The alley was fenced off.

I slammed into the chain link. What was I *thinking?* Of course it was fenced off!

I tried to climb the fence. But I was so exhausted that I couldn't even get a grip on the wire.

A pair of hands wrapped themselves around my waist. The taller man pulled me off the fence.

Seconds later, I was sitting in the construction trailer, huffing and puffing while the two men glared down at me. I was so tired and scared I couldn't even move.

"So where is it?" the short man said finally.

"Where is what?" I said glumly, trying to catch my breath.

"The tiara, obviously."

"Who knows," I said with a shrug.

"Honey," the short man said, "you need to get serious about answering my question."

"We didn't find it," I said.

The man sighed loudly. "Wrong answer, honey. Just tell us where it is, and let's get this over with," he said.

"I *don't know* where it is!" I said. "It's not there."

"Oh, it's there alright," the stocky man said. "And I think you know where it is."

The stocky man rummaged around in the drawers of the desk until he found a roll of duct tape. He pulled out a long piece—*shrreeeeeeeeeeek*—then tore it off with his teeth.

Suddenly I started to get *really* scared. Was he going to tape me to the chair or something?

"I have to go home!" I said. I tried to stand up, but the stocky man put his hand on my shoulder and pushed me back down.

"Trespassing on private property? Hacking into company computers?" the stocky man said. "I think maybe we need to call the police."

"Unless of course," the taller man said, "you want to tell us what happened to the tiara."

"I don't *know*."

The stocky man took the tape out of his mouth and reached over with it like he was about to tape me to the chair.

Before the tape touched my arm, the door opened. It was Ray D'Agostino, the construction supervisor. He stood there staring at me for a minute. His face started looking hard and angry. I thought, *Oh, no, this is only going to get worse!* I thought he was going to say something nasty to me.

But instead of talking to me, he turned to the two men and said, "What in the name of Pete are you idiots doing?"

The stocky man looked up and said, "Ray, you're not supposed to be here."

But Ray just walked across the room and said, "I asked you a question, pal. What's with the tape? What are you doing with that girl?"

The stocky man narrowed his eyes. "I don't think that's your business."

"It is when you're in my office," Ray said. "Now tell me why you're duct taping a ten-year-old child to a chair. I'm really looking forward to hearing this."

"Eleven, actually," I said.

The stocky man gave Ray a tight grin. "Taping her to the chair? You kidding me? Come on. We were just messing with her." He wadded up the piece of tape in his hand and tossed it across the room. The sticky glob stuck to the wall.

"You didn't answer my question," Ray said. "What are you doing with this kid?"

The stocky man's tight smile faded. "Okay, hold the phone, pal. Mr. Smith sent us to do a job. You don't need to know anything more than that."

"Look," Ray said, "I been a little rough on this

girl. I found her and her little friend breaking into a place that Mr. Smith said he owned. Which, it turns out, he was lying about. But as far as *I* knew, they were breaking in. And then I found them in here fooling with my computer. I didn't have any problem yelling at her for that stuff. But *guys* — c'mon! Duct tape? You can't keep her here against her will. She's a kid."

Larry — I guess that was the tall guy's name — stood up and gave Ray an intimidating look. Only, Ray didn't look all that intimidated.

"What?" Ray said, taking a step forward. "You want a piece of me?"

While the men were distracted, I took the opportunity to skooch backward in the chair a little so that the tall man's hand slipped off my shoulder.

"I'll be glad to call Mr. Smith," the stocky man said.

"I don't care what Mr. Smith says," Ray snapped. "You're getting out of here now, or I'm calling the cops."

The two men exchanged glances. Then the stocky man held up his hands like he was surrendering. "Hey, okay, whatever," he said. But then his eyes darted toward the ground, like he

was sending the bigger man some kind of signal.
As the stocky man stepped forward, distracting
Ray, the taller man balled up his fist.

The tall man pulled his fist back, looking like
he was getting ready to whack Ray. I knew I had to
do something. So without really thinking at all, I
leaned forward and sank my teeth into his arm.

You should have heard that guy scream! He was like, "*Owwwwwwww!* She bit me!"

Ray opened the trailer door and shoved the stocky man outside. "It's just you and me, Larry," he said to the tall guy.

"And *me*!" I said.

Larry rubbed his arm, winced, and said, "This ain't over, Ray."

"I don't know, Larry," Ray said. "I'm thinking maybe it is." Then he grabbed Larry by the arm and threw him out of the door like a rag doll.

Larry straightened himself up, pointed at Ray, and said, "You're finished, Ray! When we tell him what you did, Mr. Smith's gonna fire you."

"I never liked working for him that much anyway," Ray said. "Now get out of here while I'm still in a good mood." Then he slammed the door.

We watched out the window as Barrington Smith's two thugs walked away, angrily straightening their clothes.

When the two men had disappeared, Ray turned to me and said, "All right, kid, sit down and tell me what's going on here. From the beginning."

"Well," I said, "when Emma Rogers was a little girl, her mother had this tiara. . . ."

CHAPTER FIFTEEN

When I was done with my story, Ray rubbed his sun-hardened face. "You know, I was wondering why Mr. Smith was so hot to get in that house," he said. "He told me we had permission to get in there. Said there was something valuable he wanted to find. I was a little irritated to find out the guy didn't even own the house yet. And burning that stuff from the library . . . well, that just didn't sit well with me."

I looked at my watch. "My mom still owns it for another few hours. If we could find that tiara, we'd have enough money that she wouldn't have to sell out to Barrington Smith."

"Barrington Smith wouldn't be going to all this trouble if he wasn't pretty sure that tiara was in there somewhere," Ray said.

I studied his face. I still didn't really trust him. After all, he had been pretty mean to me and Hana. And he still worked for Barrington Smith.

"I know what you're thinking," he said. "Just

because I work for a guy like that doesn't mean I'm just like him. But look at it from my perspective: I thought you and your friend were trying to steal something from Mr. Smith. But it looks like he's been trying to steal something from you!"

I stared at him. Here I'd thought he was just a big, mean jerk, but it was starting to look like he wasn't. It made sense. He *had* thought Hana and I were trespassing when he found us in the Emma Rogers house. And when he caught us in the trailer? Well, let's face it, we *were* breaking into his office!

"So I have to ask you," I said. "Did you steal my locket last night?"

He looked at me with a puzzled expression. "Locket? What locket?"

And for some reason, I believed him.

"Look, kid," he said, "you want to keep living in the greatest city in the world, don't you?"

I nodded.

"Then what are we waiting for?"

"What do you mean?"

"Let's go find that tiara!"

CHAPTER SIXTEEN

I found Hana back at the house. She was bringing Daddy's tools back and giving them to my mother when Ray and I walked through the door.

"Oh, thank goodness!" Mom said, standing there in her bathrobe and her slippers. "Hana was just telling me about —"

Then she saw Ray behind me. She looked at him warily.

"Ma'am," he said, "if it's okay with you, I'd like to help your daughter find this tiara thing over in your building across the street."

"Tiara?" she said. "Look, I don't know if you know the whole story here but Zoe's a little freaked out because we're going to have to move. I'm afraid she sort of . . . invented this thing."

Ray looked at Mom for a minute. Then he shook his head.

Her eyes widened. "You seriously think there's a valuable piece of jewelry in that house?"

"Barrington Smith is pretty sure it's there,"

he said. "Say what you will about that guy, but he can smell money a mile away. And I saw the letters Emma wrote to her friend. She definitely put it in a wall of the house."

For the first time in weeks, my mom looked kind of hopeful. She pulled her bathrobe a little tighter. "Give me five minutes," she said. "I need to put some clothes on."

Normally, Mom takes even longer to get dressed than *I* do. And that's saying something! But this time she was as good as her word. Five minutes later, we were standing on the stoop of Emma Rogers's old house and Mom was fumbling with the key.

She opened the door and then looked at her watch and said, "Okay, here's the deal. My funding for this place runs out at five o'clock today. Barrington Smith already has all the papers filed. The second my claim runs out, he'll own this building. If there's really a tiara here, and it's really worth a ton of money, I'll need at least six hours to take care of all the paperwork." She looked at her watch. "We've got about two hours to find this thing. *If it's even there!*"

Ray was walking up the stoop, carrying a bunch of tools from his truck. "Then let's do it!" he said.

Hana and I started searching the drawers of all the furniture. Mom started searching the closets. And Ray started ripping out the walls. He was sure a good wall-ripper-outer. In the time it took me and Hana to rip out a three-foot-wide hole, Ray managed to bring down an entire wall.

The dust started to fill up the whole building. My throat got dry and scratchy. Hana and I had started out being really careful. But after awhile, Mom saw us and said, "Look, just start dumping everything on the floor. We can come back and sort it out later."

Upstairs, Ray was bumping and banging and smashing.

"Can we trust him?" Mom asked, pointing at the ceiling.

"He saved me from some really bad people," I said. "I think so."

"What bad people?"

"I'll tell you later," I said. Then I went into the next room and started dumping stuff on the floor. We were finding hairpins, sewing stuff, paper clips, old spoons—you name it. But no tiara.

"There was a jewelry box by her bedside table," I said. "Maybe we should check that now."

"We should finish the downstairs first, girls,"

came Mom's voice from the next room. "Let Ray finish tearing out the walls upstairs."

"Okay," I said.

"Forty-five minutes!" she added.

We kept working.

Eventually we were about done. I pulled the last drawer from a sideboard in the living room, dumped the contents on the floor and pawed through them. Match books from restaurants I'd never heard of, bits of paper with illegible notes scribbled on them, a deck of cards, a wad of dried-up rubber bands. But no tiara.

Mom walked into the room, wiping her sweating brow on her sleeve. She shook her head, looking discouraged. "Nothing?"

"Nada," I said.

"Zip," Hana said.

Ray tromped down the stairs. "I can't find anything in the walls upstairs. I'm running into trouble with all those roots, though."

"What do you mean?" Mom said.

"It's weird. There's this tree growing out of the roof. It's got roots growing inside a lot of the walls."

"We know about the tree," Mom said impatiently.

"What I'm saying, ma'am," Ray said, "is that

it's possible the tiara is somewhere in one of the walls. But the tree roots could have grown around it. If we had a month to cut all those roots open, we could find out but —" He shrugged.

Mom looked at her watch. "We've got half an hour, Ray."

"Not enough time."

"Let's just keep going," Mom said, sighing. "We'll start going through the drawers and closets upstairs. You start tearing out the walls down here. Maybe it dropped through the wall from her hiding place upstairs."

"Sounds like a plan," he said. But you could see on his face that Ray D'Agostino didn't think the tiara could have fallen through the floor.

Hana and I followed Mom upstairs.

The next few minutes were pretty much a repeat of downstairs. Only with about ten times as much dust. Hana and I were choking, and every time I saw Mom, she had streaks on her face because the dust was making her eyes water.

"Twenty minutes!" Mom called.

Hana and I went into the next room, the office. Ray had torn all the paneling off the one wall that wasn't covered with books, and the wall was bulging with black, twisty roots. Very creepy.

We went through the drawers of the desk and a low bureau with drawers. Nothing. Hana even started pulling out books.

"Maybe there's a secret door or something," she said.

But eventually we had pulled all the rotting old books off onto the floor, and there were no secret panels, no hidden rooms, no doors cleverly hidden behind the bookcase.

"Did you check that table over there?" I asked. There was one last dinky table, with one dinky drawer in it.

"No," Hana said, sounding discouraged. "I'll get it."

I heard loud footsteps thumping up the stairs.

Ray walked into the office. We looked up at him eagerly. He just shook his head and slumped down on the old leather chair behind the desk.

"Maybe it's *not* here," he said. "Maybe Mr. Smith was wrong."

Hana looked up from the drawer she'd been pawing through. "That's it," she said. "Nothing here."

Mom walked in and shook her head, too.

Mom sighed loudly. "You know, for about a tenth of a second, I kinda got my hopes up."

I looked around the room. The roots in the wall were giving me the creeps. I was ready to get out of there. In the middle was a big ball of roots where the safe had once been. It looked like a face, like some evil tree monster that —

Suddenly it hit me.

"The safe," I whispered.

"What?" Mom said.

"She must have put it in the safe."

"What safe?" Ray asked.

"Think about it," I said. "All those years, she knew that tiara was in the wall. She probably never told her parents because they'd have gotten mad at her. But once the house was hers, she probably just reached in there and pulled it out. Then she stuck it in the safe. Right?"

"You keep talking about this safe," Ray said. "But there's no safe in this house."

I pointed at the gross-looking ball of roots on the wall. "I think there is!" I said. "I bet you it's inside that ball of roots."

Ray stared at the black roots. Then his face broke into a broad smile. "Lemme go get my axe,"

he said. Then he bounded out of the room.

Hana walked up and looked at the ball of roots. "That's pretty cool looking," she said. "Looks like a face, doesn't it."

"It looks disgusting, is what it looks like!" I said.

And then Ray was back, an axe clasped in his big right hand.

He drew it back and whacked it into the ball of roots. It made a loud clang and a spark flew off the axe. "You're a genius, kid," he said to me. "I just hit metal."

Three or four more blows of his axe and the roots had dropped away. Inside was the steel door of the safe!

Mom hugged me. "You were right!" she called.

Ray turned the handle of the safe. Then his face fell. "You could be right," he said to me. "Problem is, unless you're a safe-cracker, we ain't gonna be able to find out any time soon."

We stared glumly at the safe. So close and yet so far.

"What if we just cut the whole thing out of the wall," Mom said. "We could drag it back across the street. I mean, I'd still lose the building. But if it's in there, at least it would buy me and Zoe some more time in the city while I find a job."

Ray shook his head and tapped the wall with the axe. "See these rusty looking things running down the wall? Solid steel bars. This safe's anchored in here until you knock down the whole building."

"Wait a minute! Wait a minute!" Hana said. "Remember in her letter?"

"Geniosity!" I yelled.

The two of us crawled underneath the desk and started scrabbling around in all the junk on the floor.

And then I found it—a tiny scrap of paper. I jumped up triumphantly.

"In the letter we found, Emma told her friend Ruth that her father had left a little piece of paper in his desk with the combination written on it."

Mom stared. "But that paper would have to be close to a hundred years old!"

I handed the scrap of paper to Mom. She swallowed. "You want to do the honors, hon?" she said.

I walked over to the combination dial and spun it once. Amazingly it turned easily.

"Left, twenty-one," she said.

"Left, twenty-one," I said, turning the knob until I hit the number twenty-one.

"Right, forty."

"Right, forty."

"Left, six."

"Left, six."

"Right, thirteen."

I took a deep breath.

"Right, thirteen." My heart

was beating so hard in my chest, I felt like I was going to faint. I turned the knob slowly and carefully until it came to the thirteen. I heard a soft click and my hands started to shake.

Then I reached up and pulled the handle. It moved easily. I tugged the safe open.

Everyone crowded around, trying to see inside. It took a moment for our eyes to adjust.

Then we started to cheer!

CHAPTER SEVENTEEN

<u>amous Mystery Solved!</u>

<u>Girl Discovers Priceless Tiara!</u>

_<u>Last-Minute Discovery Torpedoes Construction
Project!</u>_

I have the headlines taped on the wall over my bed now. It was kind of a big deal for a month or so. The tiara turned out to be worth a whole lot more than we expected. Enough that Mom was able to buy up the whole project from Barrington Smith.

It turned out that my Dad had made some blueprints before he died. It was kind of a fantasy, I guess, a way of imagining what he would have done with the rest of his life if he hadn't gotten cancer. Mom found the plans. Anyway, he had researched the whole block that Emma Rogers's house was on, trying to come up with a plan to restore it to what it had been like 100 years ago.

Now Mom's developing the entire block, using Dad's plans.

And her construction manager for the project? Ray D'Agostino.

<u>Me? I'm just hanging out. Just living in the Village on the best street in the best neighborhood</u> in the best city in the world.

Wow, that was pretty close - almost having to leave my home. Sometimes it's hard to explain what's so awesome about NY. But I bet if you read some pages from my journal, you'll get a good idea...

Mom told me today that she kept a scrapbook once and she's so sad it got lost. It would have been cool to look at it and see what she did and where she lived when she was young. I can't imagine growing up anywhere but New York City!!!

Probably what I like best about New York is that there's so much to see. Amazing museums (like the Natural History Museum with its huge dinosaurs) and galleries (like MOMA where even salt and pepper shakers become art). But you know me, I love simple stuff like when the steam comes up from the subway through grates in the sidewalk. And everyone ignores the signals and crosses busy streets at the same time. Plus the noise: people hailing cabs, cars honking at jaywalkers, subways rumbling, trucks clanking, something being built or torn down 24 hours a day. People speaking Russian, Spanish, English, Chinese, Yiddish, and Japanese... It's crazy. But, good crazy.

People always think Zoe is a nickname, but like what for? Zoology? Zorro? I love these two nicknames for New York the best:

The Big Apple – The first newspaper writer who used that saying got it from the racetrack where he heard stable hands saying the city was so huge and so full of promise and opportunity that they called it the "Big Apple."

THE BIG APPLE

café

The City That Never Sleeps – Day and night there are people out walking, talking, working and playing. And the restaurants and stores stay open super late and even all night!

I ♥ pizza!

You know that expression "melting pot?" It's about how people from every part of the world, every color, every religion, came here to be free. And not just 200 years ago, it's still happening! I dragged mom to Ellis Island again last week because that's where the boats would land bringing people from all over the world to find a new life in America. We went through the records and actually found my great great grandpa from when he came from Germany.

You can see the Statue of Liberty really well from Ellis Island. It was a present from France and when they brought it over by boat it was in 21 crates, in 350 pieces. It took over 4 months to put it together.

Lots of adults here don't even know how to drive because everybody walks. And if it's too far, you ride in a taxi, the bus or my favorite, the subway (also called the train). You get to push through a big turnstile, wait underground or on a big platform for the train to come and quick jump on before the doors close. Inside, everybody's squished together like sardines, but the adults don't talk to each other. Pretty funny. Our subway system is the second longest subway line in the world!

REALLY ~~BEAT~~ OLD SUBWAY TOKEN !!

Everybody loves the New York skyline with all our skyscrapers. When they built the Empire State Building it was the tallest building in the world at that time. When you stand on the street, the buildings look really gigantic.

I ♥ NY

THE 🍎 BIG APPLE

I ♥ NY
I ♥ NY
I ♥ NY
I ♥ NY
I ♥ NY

I ♥ NY
I ♥ NY

I never get tired of the rowboats in Central Park. Or ice-skating there – they have 2 rinks!!!!! Manhattan is so small, just 13 miles long and a little over 2 miles wide, with 2 million people crammed into it. We're lucky to have such a huge park running down the center of the city.

I ♥ NY
I ♥ NY

I ♥ NY
I ♥ NY

I ♥ NY

I ♥ NY
I ♥ NY

MANHATTAN
BRIDGE

BROADWAY

My mom loves Broadway plays. They're not all on the
street called Broadway, but lots of the theatres are on
that street and near it. There are 39 huge theatres for
plays and musicals. And lots of great little theatres too.
We saw "Wicked" for my 11th birthday and I loved it.
It was about the witches from The Wizard of Oz.

TAXI

BEE-
YOU-TEE-
FULL

GUITARS

Probably the thing I like best about living in Greenwich Village is Washington Square Park. Just walk through the big arch and you can see musicians, comedians, acrobats, poets — all kinds of street performers, day and night. And it's FREE! There are trees and sidewalk cafes and basketball games on 4th Street. In my little village it feels like everybody from all around the world is my neighbor.

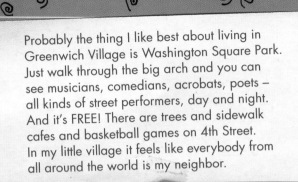

I love dressing in flea market finds and Fifth Avenue is a really cool place to get ideas. The department stores there have the wildest displays in the windows. But there's one place on Fifth Avenue no kid (or grown-up) can resist and that's FAO Schwarz, one of the biggest and coolest toy stores in the world!!!!!!!!

PIGEONS
ON THE
EMPIRE
STATE
BUILDING!

Mom should take my advice and stop cooking! We can just walk outside and get everything worth eating. In New York there are stands that sell hot dogs, pretzels, falafel, tacos, sausages, and PIZZA!!!!!!!!!